Let
Me
Breathe

Written by
Dr. MonaLisa Covington

Illustrated by
Erica J. Funderburk

To order additional copies of this book, contact:
Xlibris
844-714-8691
www.Xlibris.com
Orders@Xlibris.com

Interior Image Credit: Erica J. Funderburk

ISBN: Softcover   978-1-6641-8508-1
         Hardcover   978-1-6641-8660-6
         EBook   978-1-6641-8507-4

Print information available on the last page

Rev. date: 07/22/2021

The book begins with the story of Barry and Maggie, aka Barack and Meghan, and tells their story of friendship and devotion throughout their lives and how it intertwines with today's historical events. Not only do we get an idea of what true friendship is, but we also attain an understanding of what it means to be strong, articulate, and exhibit leadership in all facets of our lives. We also get an idea of what it takes to stand up for others when there are unjust circumstances.

The book concludes with a brief history of what others have done to promote equality, a Coronavirus prayer, and a beautiful poem. Even though the characters are "Beautiful" – African American – these messages apply to everyone as we strive to create a more just nation for all people. It was an honor to read this book!

One day at dinner, Michaela, Maggie's mother said, "Maggie, we need to have a conversation."

"What is it, Mommy?" Maggie asked.

"Maggie, we will be leaving California. I have lost my job, and we will have to return to my hometown in North Carolina," Michela said. "I have applied for and accepted a position at the North Carolina WCR Hospital."

"What about my friends?" Maggie asked. "I really like my classmates."

"You will meet new friends there," said her mom. "You are biracial; children call you names and bully you, and many days you come home crying. Your father is absent in your life, there is gun violence in schools, and there are so many little girls being kidnapped for trafficking, and this is a big state."

Maggie's eyes were large after hearing this, and she then asked, "What is trafficking, Mama?"

Sitting down, her mother answered, "Trafficking is when people kidnap children and sell their bodies, so remember, do not talk to strangers. I just want us both to be safe."

Maggie responded, "Mommy, let's pray for God to give us peace before we go to North Carolina." Maggie prayed. "God, You said, there is no right or wrong way to pray, pray from your heart. As I pray for our family as we leave California for North Carolina, please give us traveling mercy. Give us the peace to know God is with us in good and bad trouble. God loves justice and righteousness and promises that vengeance will occur in God's way and time. We sin, yet we inherit eternal life and a relationship with God when we turn to Christ. People make mistakes, complain, gossip, mistreat people of color, every day. Jesus lived a perfect life and received the opposite of fair. He was mocked, misunderstood, beaten, and killed all for me and you. It is not fair leaving, but I love and trust my Mommy. Heavenly Father, thank You that You operate out of love and mercy. And It Is So!!"

Maggie moved to North Carolina weeks later and started school at Erwin Montessori School in Greensboro, NC. It was a nice, sunny day and most kids her age were outside playing. Maggie, on the other hand, was on her porch crying. The little boy next door heard her, walked over, and sat next to her.

"Hi, my name is Barry. What's your name? Why are you crying?" Crying and snickering at the same time, Maggie replied, "I'm Maggie. I miss my dad and my friends," she said.

"I understand," Barry said. "I moved from Chicago. I will be your forever friend!"

Maggie responded, "Okay!"

For a moment Maggie was happy to have a new friend. Wiping away her tears, she looked at Barry and asked, "Where is your mask? You know we should have our faces covered because of that Covid."

"We ran out. My mom said as long as I am around the neighborhood playing outside, I should be ok. I thought it was called Coronavirus," said Barry.

"My mom said we should always have them on!" exclaimed Maggie. "I can ask my mom if we have extra."

"Ok, I will tell my mom. Do you think she might explain what the difference is?" asked Barry.

"What difference? Is there a difference?" Maggie said confused. "I don't know, but we can ask. Let's go."

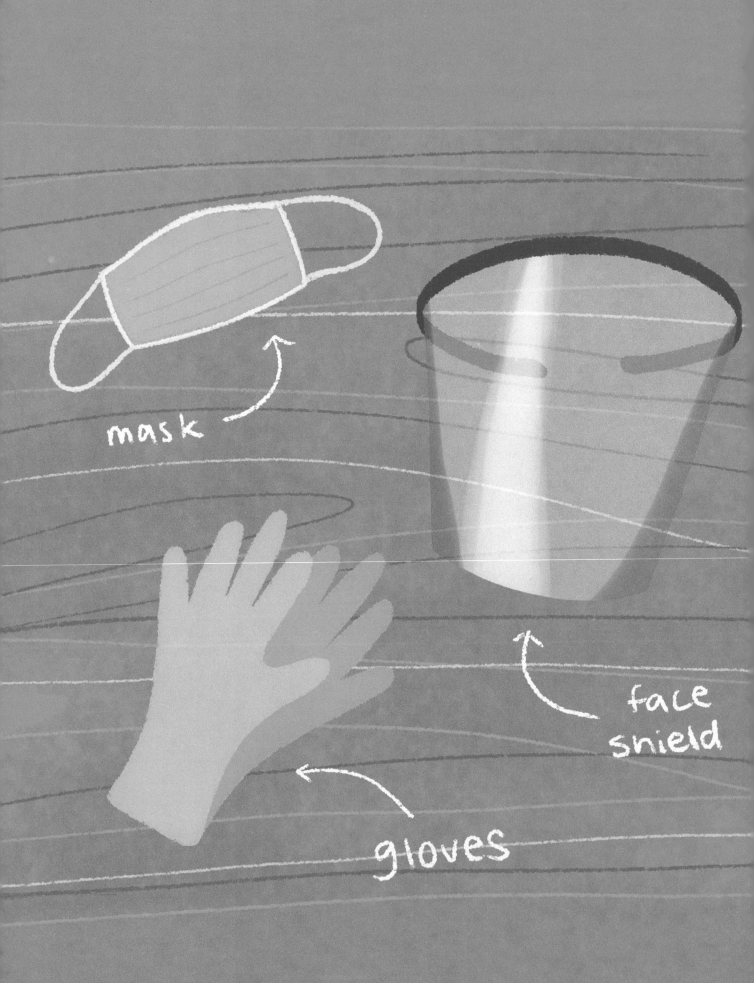

mask

face
snield

gloves

Maggie ran to her mom and asked, "Mom, what is Covid and what is Coronavirus?"

Stunned, Maggie's mom smiled, then sat them down at the table to explain. "Well, first may I ask who this little gentleman is?"

"Oh, Mom, his name is Barry. He lives next door and is my new forever friend.

"Hi, Barry! Well, it is the same disease. Covid-19 is the short version of the virus name," she explained.

"Oh, ok, yes, ma'am," said Maggie and Barry. "Also, what is PPE?" Barry asked.

"PPE is Personal Protective Equipment. A person who may be in the medical field or someone who is in touch with others like I am at the hospital has to wear it. As a Chaplain, I wear PPE to protect myself against the disease. Everyone should frequently wash his/her hands, cough in his/her elbow, stay at home, wear a mask on his/her face, and practice social distancing."

"Okay! Thanks, mom!" said Maggie.

Eventually, Maggie shared with Barry that she was biracial. "My father is wonderful (Wonderful means White or Caucasian). My mother is beautiful (Black/ African American).

Barry asked, "What do you call people of different races like Latino or Mexican?"

"They are Faithful (Foreign or Different)," said Maggie.

Barry replied, "I am biracial as well. My father is beautiful, and my mother is wonderful."

These two were inseparable. Maggie and Barry became good friends and shared everything together. They played basketball and rode their bikes. Their parents also became good friends. One day Barry and Maggie were watching TV. The death of George Floyd was on what seemed like every channel.

Sitting with Maggie and his mom, Barry asked, "Do I exist in this world or am I invisible? Why did it seem they couldn't see George Floyd or hear him. He kept saying he could not breathe, but they did not listen, and he died. This makes me think they could not see him."

Maggie then said, "Sometimes you feel as if people do not believe we exist because of the color of our skin. My mother says, 'Believe to overcome your existence. Believe in yourself or no-one else will'. She says we have beautiful and wonderful blood in our bodies." Maggie continued, "Our blood is red, but I still wonder why they hate us? What did we do? What did George Floyd and the other people who died do?"

She asked Barry's mom, "Does my life matter?"

Barry's mom looked at them and responded, "Of course, it does, and you matter to me. All lives matter. We just want black lives to matter too. You see, God says we are all one body in Christ. Jesus died on the cross for everyone, all lives, because we are all one body.

These two shared their thoughts every day. Maggie would say to Barry, "I am going to be an actress, marry a Prince and become a Princess one day!" Maggie had a wild imagination, to say the least.

Barry then said, "I am going to be the first Beautiful (Black) President of the USA! Once I am President, I will bridge the gap between hurt and hate that separates beautiful and wonderful people because I am both. I will not take sides because I believe in hope with mixed-race heritage. HOPE is believing in something before you see it. Hope is real, like faith. Faith is forsaking all and trusting God."

Maggie said silently to Barry, "I believe both our dreams will come true, and it will not matter about the color of our skin but by how smart we are."

Years had passed and the two were older now. They were both in high school. One day, Barry's aunt called his mother to inform her that his father had died. He went over to Maggie's house. She gave him hope while he cried.

A few years later, their journeys in life lead them in different directions. Maggie went to Northwestern University for Acting in Theater and Barry went to Harvard University for Law. They would always communicate by FaceTime and social media every week.

Barry, years later, met a young lady at Harvard University named Michela. She was studying law as well. She challenged him to see if he had a kind heart, good brain, had chivalry, and was respectful. He was different from any other young man she had met. Barry and Michela became remarkably close and spent all of their free time together. The two later married after law school. Barry later became a Senator for Chicago, Illinois. He went on and became the first Beautiful President of the United States. He asked, "Can We Make America better? Can we work together as one?"

With a single voice the crowd called out, "Yes, We Can!"

These words shaped Barry's reality and made him one of the most beloved Presidents of the United States. Though he was mistreated, Barry kept moving forward. He lived in hope. He became change. Barry became a role model for many brown and black children, who at one time may have never dreamed of becoming President of the United States. Barry did, and they knew that because he did, they could.

Maggie married the Prince of the United Kingdom. Marrying a brown or black person was prohibited, but she broke the mold and became the first brown Princess. Because she did, little black and brown girls all over the world now knew that they could. They had hope. Maggie was hope. Maggie became change. Hope was in the White House.

Hope was in the Palace.

In 2008, Reverend Dr. MonaLisa Covington was the first Beautiful Female Preacher to give a Dr. Martin Luther King Speech at the Municipal Hall in Reidsville, NC. The speech was well received, so there was Hope in Reidsville as a Beautiful, strong woman spoke to the crowd. Her message rang true – Yes, We Can; Yes, We Did!! Believe to Become an Achiever like President Barack Obama, Meghan Markle, and Reverend Dr. MonaLisa Covington, three remarkable Americans who are Beautiful.

Dr. King, John Lewis, and President Obama stood for Good Trouble. Standing up for their rights and the rights of all brown and black Americans drove these men to get into good trouble. Through protests and peaceful riots, these men marched for change even though most around them tried to stop them. They kept marching and because of their diligence, King and Lewis paved the way for President Barack Obama. They protested as young black Americans, and they kept the faith. They did not back down, nor were they turned around. It is this good trouble that drives our peaceful riots and demonstrations today. It is why our brown and black brothers and sisters march today.

They march for justice and for equal rights. They march for positive change.

Today these protests are done while wearing masks, but they, nonetheless, are effecting change. Change is happening in our sports leagues. Change is happening in the entertainment industry. Change is happening in our schools and on our jobs. Our marching has not been in vain, but because racism still exists, we still have a long way to go. We cannot stop; we must keep marching. We must stay in Good Trouble. We will not just talk but stand together in unity, peace, love, and stand for justice.

While Barry was sitting in the foyer waiting to speak with his pastor, Dr. Hughes, he overheard his pastor's conversation with Rev. Milton on the telephone in the church office: "The clergies are going to protest and have a rally in Elizabeth City next month for Marcus Brown, who was shot in the head by police officers as his car was moving in his driveway."

Maggie, I know some of the clergies like Drs. Barber, Spearman, Carver, and Revs. Johnson, Allen, and Drumwright. I know Dr. Carver spoke on Spectrum News; he was born in Elizabeth City where Marcus Brown was killed by the police and was a minister at Genesis Baptist Church. He was a black, brown little boy like me once. Barry asked Maggie, "I thought a police officer's job was to serve, protect, and save lives, not be a murderer. I once wanted to be a police officer to protect our community."

Barry and Maggie believe in Faith, Love, and Hope like Dr. Corbett. George Floyd said, "I Can't Breathe."

Barry and Maggie said, "Police Officers, Let Me Breathe. Black Lives Matter, Let Me Breathe, and Let My People Go!"

Maggie said, "I heard on the news yesterday that President Joe Biden signed a bill, on Thursday, June 17, 2021, to make Juneteenth a Federal Holiday commemorating the end of slavery in the United States.

Barry said, "Maggie, why do you watch the news all the time?"

"So, I can be knowledgeable and keep you up to date on what is happening in this world and our lives."

"Thanks," said Barry. "Oh, by the way, what does Juneteenth mean and who is Ms. Opal Lee?"

"Juneteenth marks when freedom and racial equality was declared 150 years ago because of slavery and racial bias in criminal justice for African Americans in Galveston, Texas." Juneteenth is a celebration for 'Good Trouble' that Dr. Martin Luther King, Jr. and Congressman John Lewis started saying.

Ms. Opal Lee was called the 'grandmother of the movement' to make Juneteenth a federal holiday. Biden at one point left the stage and walked over to the 94-year-old to speak with her directly. Vice President Kamala Harris, the first Black Vice President, also gave Lee her due in her remarks, saying, "And looking out across this room, I see the advocates, the activists, the leaders, who have been calling for this day for so long, including the one and only Ms. Opal Lee."

Barry said, "President Obama and Dr. Covington said, 'Yes, We Can', and Yes We Did."

Barry and Maggie both said, now we can say, "Let Me Breathe."

Dr. Anthony Fauci, the National Disease Expert, gives some recognition to some who look like us. We are soooooo proud that a young, Beautiful (Black African American) lady helped develop the CoronaVirus Vaccine. She is a 34-year-old woman who graduated from UNC Chapel Hill in North Carolina and is a brown color like us. She received her B.S. in Biological Sciences, with a secondary major in Sociology, in 2008 from the University of Maryland – Baltimore County, then got her Ph.D. in Microbiology and Immunology in 2014 at the University of North Carolina at Chapel Hill.

Dr. Kizzmekia Corbett is a close friend of the team leader for the virus, Dr. Barney Graham. According to a report, Dr. Corbett is the lead scientist for coronavirus vaccine research at the National Institute of Medicine. Boys and Girls, look in the mirror and speak positive things about your life. Say things like, I am smart, I am intelligent, I am beautiful, and I am going to allow God, my parents, and Dr. Corbett to give me HOPE. Having Only Positive Experiences. Hope at times is all we have to cling to. Hope keeps us going. Maggie and Barry kept going. Boys and girls, you keep going too.

Boys and Girls go boldly in the direction of your dream to live the life you can only imagine, becoming who you are. Dream It, Imagine It, Speak It, Believe It, Change It, Achieve It to Become It!

Dr. Kizzmekia Corbett

Boys and Girls go boldly in the direction of your dream to live the life you can only imagine, becoming who you are. Dream It, Imagine It, Speak It, Believe It, Change It, Achieve It to Become It!

Coronavirus Prayer

God is Our Protector; we shall not be afraid.
God give us peace in the midst of Corona,
God guides us in the paths of power uncertainties.
Even when we walk is dark place of fear, God is with Us.
We will not fear no evil with Corona God is with Us.
Corona, Rona, Pandemic, Virus Jesus' Blood Comfort Us.
God gives strength in suffering of virus of enemies' imps,
Plot evil devises, schemes, Lysol vaccine, sickness,
attaches cannot overcome
Jesus' Blood on the Cross.
God gives us vaccines through researchers, not
Lysol chemical and anoints our heads with
oil and our bodies overflows with healing.
This earth is Gods and everything that dwells in this world
for Us to vision the goodness and love of God will deliver
us from this pandemic all the days of our lives.
Gods' goodness and mercy shall follow Us from this a
afflictions during despairs to listen to the voice and cry
for His help as we seek and turn our faces to the Lord,
The Lord is Shepherd of this world, not the Mayor,
Governor nor President but God is more than a Conquer,
we shall dwell in Presence of the Lord forever.

We are different on the outside but the same on the inside.

We are beautiful, wonderful, and marvelous made in the Image of One.

We are black like coal and sparkle like a diamond.

We are white like a pearl in a shell.

We are foreign like a rainbow of color, all blended into One.

We are the Broken, Hope, Chosen, Love that Becomes.

We are not divided but blended with Peace.

We will inhale hate and exhale love.

We will inhale division and exhale Unity.

We will inhale violence, exhale Healing.

We will inhale guns and exhale hugs.

We will inhale bullies and exhale friendship.

We will inhale trafficking and exhale togetherness.

We will inhale disrespect and exhale respect, for one another.

We will inhale Doubt and exhale Destiny.

CPSIA information can be obtained
at www.ICGtesting.com
Printed in the USA
BVHW021007310821
615693BV00002B/52